The Goodbye Book

TOdd PaRR

Megan Tingley Books
LITTLE, BROWN AND COMPANY
New York   Boston

It's hard to say goodbye to someone.

You might not know what to feel.

You might be very sad.

You might be very mad.

You might not feel like talking to anyone.

You might just feel like hiding.

Things might not seem fun anymore.

You might not feel like eating.

You might not feel like sleeping.

You might try to stop thinking about it.

You might pretend it didn't happen.

You might be confused.

But eventually you'll start to feel better.

You'll remember how you laughed.

You'll remember all the fun you had.

You'll have days when you feel up
and days when you feel down.

You'll remember all the special times.

You'll remember everything
you learned together.

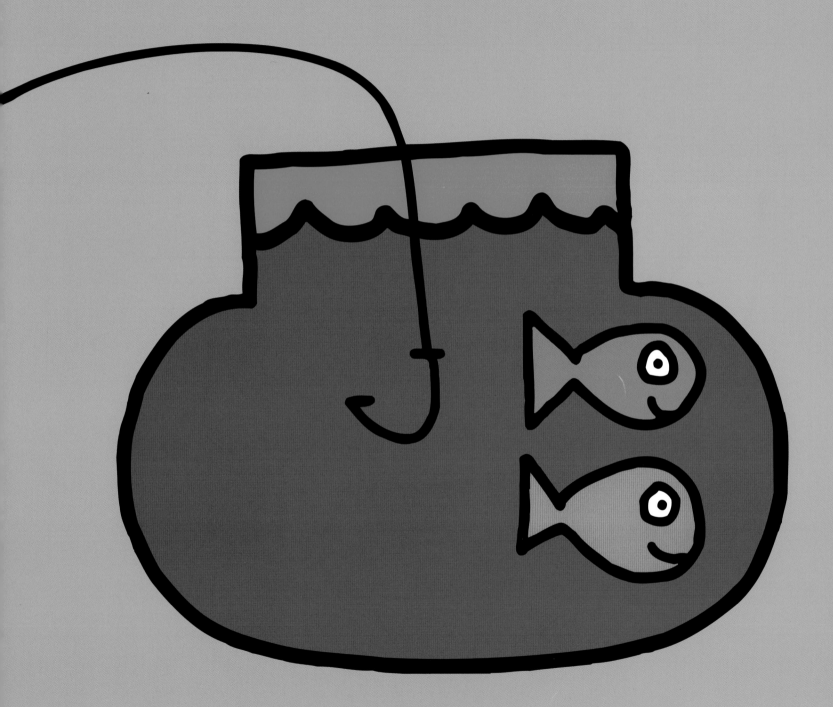

You might feel like talking to someone.

You might even feel like drawing a picture.

You might wonder where they went
or what they are doing now.

Most of all, you'll remember how much
you love and miss them.

You'll go on and try to be brave.

And you'll remember that there will always be someone to love you and hold you tight.

We all get sad when we say goodbye to someone we love. Always try to remember all the happy times you shared together.

The End.

Love, Todd

Of all my books, this was the hardest to write—
because it's never easy to say goodbye.

Love, Todd

This book was edited by Liza Baker, Megan Tingley, and Allison Moore and designed by Saho Fujii.
The production was supervised by Erika Schwartz, and the production editor was Wendy Dopkin.

• Little, Brown and Company • Hachette Book Group • 1290 Avenue of the Americas, New York, NY 10104 • Visit us at lb-kids.com • Little, Brown and Company is a division of Hachette Book Group, Inc. The Little, Brown name and logo are trademarks of Hachette Book Group, Inc. • The publisher is not responsible for websites (or their content) that are not owned by the publisher. • First Edition: September 2015 • Library of Congress Cataloging-in-Publication Data • Parr, Todd, author, illustrator. • The goodbye book / Todd Parr. — First edition. • pages cm • "Megan Tingley Books." • Summary: Illustrations and brief text relate how a person might feel when they lose someone they love. • ISBN 978-0-316-40497-6 (hc) — ISBN 978-0-316-40495-2 (ebook) [1. Loss (Psychology)—Fiction.] I. Title. • PZ7.P2447Goo 2015 • [E]— dc23 • 2014010658 • 10 9 8 7 6 5 4 3 2 1 • SC • PRINTED IN CHINA